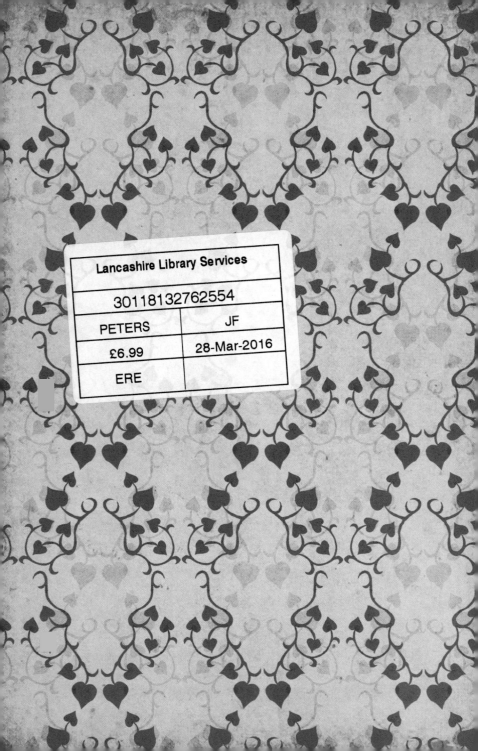

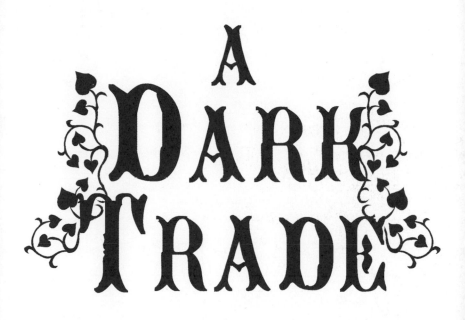

A DARK TRADE

First published in 2016 in Great Britain by
Barrington Stoke Ltd
18 Walker Street, Edinburgh, EH3 7LP

www.barringtonstoke.co.uk

Text © 2016 Mary Hooper

A CIP catalogue record for this book is available
from the British Library upon request

ISBN: 978-1-78112-516-8

Printed in China by Leo

A Dark Trade

MARY HOOPER

Barrington Stoke

# CHAPTER I

I couldn't help but gasp when Mrs Parkins and I reached Rose Villa, the house where I was to begin work as a kitchen maid. It stood tall and elegant in a pretty garden square filled with trees, shrubs and some late-blooming flowers. It was five floors high and at the first floor was a balcony with a row of bay trees. Behind the bay trees I could see large windows with ruffled and draped curtains, and two oil lamps which gave a soft glow to the room within.

"I am to live *here* ...?" I said to Mrs Parkins in amazement, as I stared up at the place in all its glory. The orphanage where I'd lived until then had been a squat building of dark brick, with small windows striped with iron bars and dull slates on its roof. The yard where we took our outside exercise contained nothing, no plant, tree, flower or growing thing.

Mrs Parkins was a matron at the orphanage and I was in her care that day. She tugged at my arm. "Come along!" she snapped. "Don't stand there gawking, girl!"

I let her pull me along, past the white marble steps up to the glossy black front door, and around to the back of the house. Here was a cobbled yard with two smart carriages, a handcart and three horses looking out of stable doors.

The back of the house wasn't as elegant as its perfect white front, but there was busyness and bustle. Dogs were running about and several women in blue aprons were going about their duties with piles of white sheets, silver trays and flowers. No one took any notice of us or even looked in my direction. 'Well,' I thought, 'I'm used to that.'

"Down you go," Mrs Parkins said, and she prodded me over to the basement stairs. "What are you waiting for?"

"So this is the girl, is it?" Mrs Green the housekeeper asked. She felt my upper arms, then looked at my teeth in the way I've seen carters examine the inside of a horse's mouth. She nodded and muttered. "Have you instructed her as to a kitchen servant's duties?"

"Oh, of course, Madam," Mrs Parkins assured her. "I trained her myself."

I looked round. I didn't know then, but this room was the housekeeper's parlour. I could see it didn't have such lavish furniture as the front rooms I'd seen from the road, but it was still a hundred times nicer than any room I had ever been in before. I couldn't help standing there and staring about me – at the heavy curtains with golden fringes, at the china ornaments crammed into the cabinet and the majestic portrait of our Queen, Victoria, above the fireplace.

Mrs Green nodded at me but spoke to Mrs Parkins. "And how long has she been at the orphanage?" she asked.

"Since she was born," was the reply.

"Really? Do you know the circumstances?"

"Some," Mrs Parkins said. "It seems a young woman was taken into an East London workhouse, very ill. A bit later they found this one ..." she jerked her thumb at me ... "in a bundle of rags on the steps outside. She was a –" She mouthed the next word, but of course I knew what it was.

Mrs Green just shrugged, as much as to say that this wasn't unusual.

"The young woman died before they could make her give her name," Mrs Parkins said. "We took her baby into our orphanage. Now she's sixteen she should have gone into the parish workhouse, but your master and mistress have been so kind as to offer a place for a homeless girl."

Mrs Green and Mrs Parkins looked at each other. I knew – and they both knew – that it was not a kind act at all. Girls like me were ten a penny, all willing to work for almost nothing in order to keep out of the workhouse.

"She started on domestic duties when she was seven years old," Mrs Parkins put in. "She's very willing."

"She needs to be." Mrs Green walked all round me, looking me up and down. "There are twelve servants in the house, and seven members of the family. A kitchen maid will have to fetch and carry for everyone."

"Of course," Mrs Parkins said.

"What's her name?"

"Her name is Georgina Friday."

"A strange name ..." Mrs Green said.

"Mr *George* Scribbs admitted her on a *Friday* night," Mrs Parkins explained. "He was one of the workhouse beadles. We call her Gina in the orphanage."

Mrs Green sniffed. "She'll be called by her surname here."

"As you wish." Mrs Parkins poked me in the back again. "Speak up, girl. Tell Mrs Green how grateful you are to be given the chance to work."

I cleared my throat ready to make the little speech Mrs Parkins had taught me, but Mrs Green wasn't interested. She turned to Mrs Parkins again. "You can be sure that if Friday doesn't suit us – if she's not honest and hard-working – then we will reprimand her severely and return her to you."

I didn't know the meaning of this word – *reprimand* – but I didn't like the sound of it. I thought it must be something unpleasant. Still, I was happy to be away from the orphanage and I decided there and then that I would work hard and be honest and all the other things they wanted. That way, I could hope that I'd never set foot inside the miserable and mouldy walls of an orphanage or a workhouse ever again.

I thought I might feel tearful when I said goodbye to Mrs Parkins, or that she might have been a little sad, but she just patted me on the arm and said I must try and be a credit to the orphanage.

"Obey orders, work hard and respect the family," she said. "They have taken you into their home." Then she looked me in the eye and added, "Remember, your new life starts from today. Don't waste it."

# CHAPTER 2

"Georgina Friday! You never went and did it!" Jameson, the boot boy, hooted with laughter.

I stared at him, confused. "But you told me ..."

"Yeah, but it was a joke!"

We had all gathered for breakfast in the servants' dining room at Rose Villa. Mrs Green banged the table for order. "What's going on here?" she asked. "What's all this about?"

"Please, Mrs Green," I began. "Jameson told me there was a mouse on the loose. He said I should hide under the table in the breakfast room and be ready to catch it before anyone in the family saw it."

I looked around and saw that everyone in the room was smirking.

"So what happened?" Mrs Green asked.

"I got under the table and the family all came in, one by one, and I didn't see any mice. I stayed there because I was scared to come out, and then Miss Lutterworth looked under the table and found me and ..."

There was an outburst of giggles which made my cheeks flush with shame.

"Well, don't you take the biscuit, Friday!" Jameson said. "Fresh from the orphanage and as green as a sprout."

"Green as a whole barrow-load of sprouts!" said Williams the gardener. Everyone laughed even louder. Even the butler's straight line of a mouth twitched at the corners.

"Do you always believe what you're told, Friday?" Mrs Green asked.

"Well, sometimes ..." I murmured.

"Last week there was the episode with the bootblack around your eyes," she said.

I hung my head. That was Jameson again – he'd told me to have a look through Mr

Lutterworth's binoculars. What he hadn't told me was that he'd smeared the eye pieces with black stuff, and this had smudged all round my eyes. None of the servants told me about it, but they all grinned every time they saw me. And then I went into the housekeeper's parlour and saw my face in the little mirror on her shelf. I looked a grubby mess, as if I'd been in a brawl in the street.

That morning in the kitchen I sat down at the end of the bench. Everyone else seemed to have served themselves, so I reached for the pot to help myself to porridge.

"Aren't you forgetting something, Friday?" Mrs Green said. Her voice was very clipped.

I looked around. Everyone was tucking in to their breakfasts.

"You must clean and scour the upstairs chamber pots while the family are eating," she said.

"But I've been busy in the ..." I began.

"I know where you've been, Friday – playing mice under the breakfast table."

The others all began laughing again, and Mrs Green clapped her hands. "*Now*, please!" she said. "The master and mistress don't want to go up to their rooms and meet last night's chamber pots coming down."

I bobbed a curtsey and went. If there was any porridge left it would be claggy and cold by the time I returned.

The chamber pot task wasn't the most pleasant. There were eight of them and I had to take each one outside and tip its contents on the heap of earth and ashes beside the stables. After that I had to take them to the scullery and clean them with boiling water, scour them with sand and return them to their proper rooms, sparkling clean. It *was* a task done by the lowliest member of staff, but I'd believed Jameson when he told me about the mouse and so I thought someone else would have done it for me. They were right – I *was* as green as a bucket full of sprouts.

I suppose I was the youngest servant and the last to arrive at Rose Villa, and I should have expected the others to play tricks on me. But at the orphanage there had been no such pranks. We were all much too scared by the sight of the

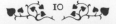

heavy wooden stick which hung in the hallway and which the staff used at the least excuse. And there was one other big difference – at the orphanage no one had parents, and so we learned to stick together as a family against those who were in charge.

But in Rose Villa it was everyone for themselves. Servants told tales on one another and spoke behind one another's backs to try to gain favour with the family. Weasel-faced Jameson seemed to find a special joy in making me look stupid in front of others.

I'd been there for about three weeks and was still awkward and out of place when I noticed that Master Lutterworth was giving me the glad eye. Now, I've not had much to do with lads, but sometimes in the street or market place a boy has winked at me and I've smiled back at him. These looks and winks, of course, were from lads of my own sort – errand boys and boot boys, street lads and fruit sellers. I knew straight away that this attention from Master Lutterworth was going to mean trouble for me.

I had only come face to face with him once or twice – when he appeared in the servants' hall to look for his valet or came down with a pair of muddy boots for Jameson to clean. Every time, he'd leer at me or make a lewd comment about my legs or my figure. Sometimes he'd hide behind a doorway and try to grab me as I went past. I didn't welcome his attention in the slightest – the comments *or* the wandering hands. And so I did my best to avoid being alone with him. If he made coarse remarks, I'd pretend I hadn't heard them. Master Lutterworth was a few years older than me, and was, of course, the first son of a very well-to-do family and the product of a good education. Any flirting on my part was out of the question – I wouldn't have *dared*.

This was the right way to behave, I realised, when I told one of the other kitchen maids about the way he was acting.

Stoner was a few years older than me – and not a bit surprised to hear about Master

Lutterworth. "You must watch out for that one," she told me. "He's a bad lot."

"Has he said anything to you, then?" I asked. "Anything he shouldn't have done?"

"No," she said. She lowered her voice. "But we had a young kitchen maid here last year – name of Parsons – and he took a fancy to her. She was a lovely girl, the bonniest face you ever saw, green eyes and a blaze of copper-red hair."

"And what happened?" I asked.

"Can't you guess?" she said. "He forced himself onto her, and before long she found herself with child."

I gasped.

"Of course, the family refused to believe it was his baby," Stoner said. "Poor Parsons and her bairn ended up on the streets."

I was shocked. "I promise you I have no intention of misbehaving ..." I began. I was thinking of my *own* poor start in life, but Stoner cut in.

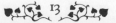

"Don't be so sure, my girl," she said, and her voice was stern. "Don't forget that they are the masters and we are the servants. They provide our food, clothing and the roof over our heads. If they want something, most times they get it."

# CHAPTER 3

Stoner's stark warnings and her story of Parsons and her poor baby unsettled me, but life at Rose Villa wasn't all bad.

The best thing about working there was where the house stood – in the centre of London and, it seemed to me, the very centre of life itself. The orphanage had stood among fields and woods and farms in the country, far from railway and stage-coach routes. This was in order to stop those who might think of running away (which we often did). There were no shops, markets or fairs near by – and none of us had any money to enjoy such pleasures even if there had been. The orphanage was as bleak and forlorn outside as in.

Rose Villa, on the other hand, was a bustle of activity. It was close to a lane of shops and we had a local market. Every day the butcher, dairyman, baker and greengrocer would knock

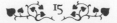

on the back door to take orders from Mrs Parkins.

I was often sent out on errands, to buy goods for the house or to get the *Sporting Review* newspaper for the butler. I'd never had such freedom before, because at the orphanage we'd only been allowed out with a minder. Boys who did run off (it was usually the boys) were nearly always caught. To punish them, the staff would give them six whacks of the heavy stick that hung in the hall and then handcuff them to their bunks for a week.

One morning about eight weeks after I'd come to live at Rose Villa, I had a bit of a set-to with Master Lutterworth and so I was very keen to get out of the house. I'd gone into his room at the normal time to collect his chamber pot, only to find – to my horror – that he was still in bed. *Still in bed*, despite the fact the gong had been struck a good ten minutes ago and the master and mistress were already at breakfast.

"Oh! I beg your pardon, sir ..." I stammered, and I began to back out of the room. "I didn't realise ..."

"Don't apologise," he said. "I stayed in bed in order to see you." He swung his bare legs out of the covers.

"I'll come back later!" I said, and backed away faster.

"No. Stay!" I'd almost got to the door when he reached and grabbed me. "I have a favour to ask of you, Friday," he said, and his hot hand twisted into mine.

"Please, sir," I stammered. "I'll send up your valet if you want something done. He's just having breakfast."

"I wouldn't want Reeves to grant this favour!" he said. "Can't you guess what it is?"

I turned my face away. "No, sir, I can't."

"Just one little kiss, Friday. That's all."

"No, sir!" I said, and my face flushed red with anger. "Please don't speak to me of such things."

"No one will know," he said. "Surely you're not so mean as to refuse me one kiss."

"One kiss might lead to something else," I said, and I did my best to get out of his grasp.

"And what if it does?"

"Then it could mean disaster for a poor kitchen maid," I said. I was thinking of the young girl with red hair that Stoner had told me about.

"Are you trying to tell me how to behave, you cheeky young madam!" Master Lutterworth said.

"No, sir, I ..."

He made another lunge to grab me again, but I ducked and pulled away from him, and he fell against the wardrobe and knocked his head.

"How dare you!" he cried. He looked crumpled and silly in his nightshirt. "Come back here!"

But by then I was out of the door and half way down the stairs.

"You wait! I *will* have what I want!" was his final shot.

I was shaken and full of dread, but I was also too scared to say anything to the other staff downstairs in case they thought I'd led Master Lutterworth on in some way. I would have told Stoner, but she was nowhere to be seen. When Mrs Green told me I must go out and run a few errands, I was very happy to go. I needed to think about what I was going to do, and how I was going to handle Master Lutterworth.

I didn't doubt that he would persist with his attempts on me. When he did, I could either give in, lose my honour and perhaps have a child, or refuse him – and that would risk making him so angry that he'd take his revenge and have me sent back to the orphanage.

Whatever happened, I couldn't think how there could be any good end to it, at least not for me.

When I got to the local market, I found the few things I'd been sent for. Then, since I knew Mrs Green was going to be busy most of the morning, I decided to go a little further into the city.

I took a path which led past St Giles' Church and the old, bad place where the Great Plague had begun many years ago. Many thousands of people had died here and it was still a desperately poor area. Shacks and makeshift houses huddled along the mean streets and all were in a very poor state. Some were built higgledy-piggledy on top of each other, others had bits of wood instead of glass in their windows and pieces of cloth stuffed into cracks to try and keep out the cold. Soon, they said, these old houses would come down so they could begin to build an underground railway.

Thin, pale children played in the gutters. Most of them wore little more than rags, yet I found that I envied their freedom. They were poor, grubby and hungry, but I'd rather have spent my childhood like them, with a family and the freedom to come and go as they wished. Better that than be trapped in an orphanage where children were beaten for the smallest mischief.

I sighed. When I'd left the orphanage I'd thought my life was going to be different, better. Now I had the problem of Master Lutterworth and the sly tricks played by Jameson, and I could see that life at Rose Villa was going to present just as many difficulties as life in the orphanage had done. I was still at everyone's beck and call. I still had to dance to the tunes that others played.

Having come to this sorry conclusion, I forced myself to put dismal thoughts aside and enjoy my freedom and the life all around me. I watched the peddlers with their bright ribbons and hair ornaments, the quack doctors with their "cures for any ill", the balladeers singing the latest songs – and I took pleasure in them all.

When I reached Cheapside, I turned into a small lane of shops – very poor ones, with makeshift stalls or tables set up outside. Two or three sold food – sprats, half-penny ices or baked potatoes. In the grimy windows of others I could see a mish-mash of items for sale – kitchen tools, firewood and rat poison.

I had no money to spend, for I would not get my wages until I'd been at Rose Villa half a year, but still I stared into the shop at the very end of the parade. It had three plate-glass windows, and each was crammed with an amazing selection of old clothing. Clothes hung inside and out, pegged along washing lines or dangling from hangers, each garment fighting with the others for space.

I knew the clothes would be third- or fourth-hand, and most of them were a sludgy grey colour as a result of the dozens of times they had been washed and rewashed. There were small hand-written notices stuck messily on the window. As I went closer to read them, I thanked the orphanage for teaching me one useful skill.

FOR SALE AND HIRE

Mourning Clothes for Funerals.

Paris fashions from the FRENCH Designers.

Wear Russian velvet for total Elegance.

I was riveted by the huge amount of clothes on display in the main window. None seemed as if they might be the high fashions promised, but still I began to think about what I'd need for the winter. I'd have to have a new coat, that was for sure, for I only had the one which had been part of my orphanage uniform. It was grey with a band of dark red around the hem and it said *Orphanage Child* as clearly as if the words had been written on the back. Perhaps I could ask my employers to pay some of my wages early so I could buy a coat?

As I turned away I saw another notice.

SMART LAD WANTED – APPLY WITHIN.

I stared at it with a frown. It wasn't fair! The boys always got the best jobs! Why couldn't a smart *girl* do the same thing? I was willing to bet that a girl working in this shop could do anything a boy could do – and how much nicer than Rose Villa it would be. No Master Lutterworth, no chamber pots to scour, no other servants to boss me around!

I was thinking about this when a group of young boys of eight or nine years old ran into the lane with a cardboard box they were kicking around. They saw me on my own, and of course they thought I was fair game for a bit of teasing. They began to circle around me, and every so often one darted towards me and gave me a tweak or a tickle. They meant no harm, I knew that – it was only a game. But I was in a strange mood after that morning's encounter with Master Lutterworth, and that was enough to make me turn on them with a sudden roar and a stream of swear words I'd learned from the orphanage boys.

Even this didn't shock them, and they ran off down the lane, laughing. They found another victim there – a girl who was begging. She held a bowl out to collect money in one hand and had a white stick in the other.

These odds didn't seem fair – one blind girl versus a raggedy crowd of street urchins. I was about to run up there and see them off when a stout man came around the corner with a horse and cart. The moment they saw him, the urchins scattered in different directions.

"Over here!" the man barked, and the girl turned towards the voice, so that I could see her face. She was about my age, I suppose, but smaller and more delicate, with glossy dark hair tumbling over her shoulders. Her eyes were closed and her pale face was blank.

"In yer get," the brute told her. He didn't help her into a seat in the cart, but instead gripped her arm and shoved her towards the back, so that she stumbled and fell onto the floor.

I wanted to protest, to run and help her up onto the seat, but then I looked at the size of the man I took to be her father. He had massive shoulders and a neck as thick as a bulldog's, and I didn't dare cross him. He whipped the horse and I flinched. Then they trundled off down the lane.

I began to walk towards Rose Villa. I was fuming as I thought to myself how unjust it all was. It seemed to me that men – boys – had it much easier than girls. Life, in all its aspects, was so much better for boys.

And then I thought about the scribbled note in the window – *SMART LAD WANTED* – and a sudden idea came to me. Why couldn't I be that smart lad? *Why didn't I pretend to be a boy?*

# CHAPTER 4

I might not have taken this daring idea any further but then I got back to Rose Villa and I was scolded three times by Mrs Green.

First, it seemed that I had not cleaned the silverware well enough the day before.

Second, I had taken too long over that morning's errands.

And third, I had used the family's stairs when I had been told again and again to only *ever* use the back stairs.

It was Jameson who told Mrs Green about this last crime, for I saw the sly smile on his face and the way he winked at one of the valets as Mrs Green ticked me off.

Mrs Green made me stay up that night after the rest of my tasks were done and re-polish the silver candlesticks and cutlery with emery powder. This took more than three hours and gave my hands such a stinging rash that, when at last I got to bed, I couldn't sleep for the pain.

I lay awake with my hands on fire and Stoner snoring away beside me, and I thought more about my idea. Could I *really* change myself into a boy? I'd need a new name, new clothes, a new place to live. Was it possible that I could get these things?

'No,' I thought. 'Of course not.'

But *then* I thought about Master Lutterworth and the way he'd stayed in his bed in order to leap out and grab me. He was bound to try the same thing again. For how long would I be able to fight him off? The thought of being cornered by him, the idea of his hands running over me, made me shudder.

That morning I had asked Stoner – who was always full of advice – what would happen if a maid ran away from the family she worked for. Stoner knew right away that I was talking about myself. She said that if I was caught I'd be in Big Trouble. She went on to explain that the Lutterworth family would have paid a sum to the orphanage for my services for the next four years. If I left before then, every constable in the city would come to hunt me down.

"I've seen a girl tied behind a cart and whipped through the streets for running away," Stoner said.

"They'd have to catch me first!" I said.

She shook her head. "Tis our lot in life to serve our betters," she reminded me. "And the sooner you knuckle down to do just that, the more content you'll be."

<hr>

As I lay in bed and thought it all over, the grandfather clock in the hall began to strike. I counted the chimes. *Three o'clock!* Three o'clock in the morning and I had to be up at five to rake the ashes out of the kitchen range, chop the wood and lay up the downstairs fires. Unless ...

Before I was even aware of what I was doing, I'd climbed out of the old iron bed. As Stoner snuffled and snored, I pulled on my skirt and top, picked up my boots and crept down to the kitchen. There was a lobby by the back door where Jameson slept under the shelves of outdoor shoes. By the light of the kitchen fire I could see his sleeping form there, huddled under a blanket. He had put his clothes – a pair of rough trousers, coarse linen shirt and dark jacket – on the top shelf. I quietly opened the lobby door, removed these items and carried them into the housekeeper's parlour.

I'm tall for a girl – almost the same height as Jameson – and with my boots on and a piece of string to hold up the trousers, his clothes fitted me very well. My hair might have been a problem, but before Mrs Parkins had brought me to Rose Villa, she had cut it short and told me that it would be less prone to lice that way. "Or to attract servant boys," I'd heard her mutter. Now I wetted it and flattened it down, then found an old tweed cap to fit me.

I looked at the finished result in Mrs Green's mirror. Not bad! I was a different person. A smart lad indeed ...

I put my skirt, top and petticoat onto the shelf above Jameson. When he woke up, he'd either have to put these on or appear in front of the maids stark naked. I felt a bit guilty when I thought of how everyone would laugh at him, but then I reminded myself of how he'd always been unkind to me, and the guilt didn't last long.

CHAPTER 5

It was still dark when I opened the back door and let myself out. One of the horses gave a snicker as I passed its stable, and somewhere far off I could hear a cat wailing, but there was no other sound.

As I crept across the cobbles towards the street, I kept as close as possible to the shadow cast by the garden wall. I heard, some way off, the call of the night watchman. *"Half past three o'clock on a fine night and all's well!"*

I took several deep breaths. All was well, so far.

By the time I'd walked right into the city the watchman was calling that it was five o'clock, and there were workers appearing on the streets. The crossing-sweepers came first, with brooms in hand ready to clear paths through the dirt for the housewives going shopping. Then I saw mudlarks with their tin buckets, on their way to see what they could find in the mud on the river shore. The mudlarks were mostly raggedy boys – digging in the mud and filth was hard and dirty work, even when the sun was shining. Close on their heels came little girls with bunches of watercress to sell, peddlers hoping to get a good pitch, and boys trudging along the gutters in bare feet, picking up cigar and cigarette ends which had been thrown away the day before.

I used this time to try to walk more like a boy. I'd already noticed that girls walked with their heads down, took small steps and were careful to avoid banging into other people, while boys took a firmer, more jaunty pace, had a swagger and looked passers-by in the eye. After I had observed the manner of a few apprentice boys, I stuck my hands in my pockets, lifted my chin and began to say a brisk "Good morning" to those I passed. Between these greetings, I tried to teach myself to whistle. This was, I thought, a very boyish thing to do – but quite hard to get the hang of.

I came to a baker's shop and stopped to practise what I was going to say before I went in. I'd made the fortunate discovery of a penny in the hem of Jameson's trousers.

"Cottage loaf, please," I asked in the deepest voice I could muster. It sounded odd and false to me, but no one in the shop bothered to look round at me.

"That'll be one penny, sir," the girl behind the counter said as she handed me the bread.

I tucked it under my arm and felt brave enough to try a few more words. "They do say the day will be warm."

"Then I hope you enjoy it, sir," she said. She put her head on one side and smiled such a coy smile at me that I could only think she was flirting with me.

I grinned at this idea as I walked to one of the market squares and sat on the steps of a fountain to eat my loaf. I found that I was starving, and – since I was dressed as a boy and had a boy's appetite – I didn't pause to eat the bread in dainty bites, but broke chunks from it and crammed them into my mouth just as the apprentice boys did. When my meal was over, I stood up and slapped my legs in a manly way to shake off the crumbs I'd made. I was learning fast. I was George now, not Gina.

It was not easy to find the old clothes shop again, for the city was a mass of little lanes and streets which curled back on themselves or led into dead ends. I walked and walked and, as I did so, I worked out what I was going to say about my background, what story I should tell.

At last I found the shop again and pushed my way past its rows of old frocks, piles of shirts and hangers dangling with skirts and petticoats. But I discovered that the shopkeeper was not at all interested in where I'd come from or what I'd done in the past. He had no need to know my story.

He was a short, plump man, bald except for a greasy streak of hair which lay flat across the top of his head.

"What I want is a lad who can be discreet," he said. "Know what that word means, do you?"

"Yes, sir," I said. "A person who can stay in the background." I'd had plenty of experience of that.

He nodded. "I want a smart lad who can disappear when he has to. Someone who can turn his hand to most things. Who can drive a cart, look after the shop and make sure customers part with their money."

"That sounds just like me, sir!" I said. I was so eager that I almost forgot to speak in my deeper voice. This new life sounded very appealing. One person to boss me about would be a lot better than twelve.

"You'd have to live on the job," the man said. "Sleep under the counter, like."

"That'd suit me very well."

"You'll find the lavatory and tap in the yard," he went on. "No regular hours. And I can only pay you a pound a month."

"That would be quite all right, sir."

"Yes. I daresay it is. And none of this 'sir'. Me name's Threads."

"Right you are, Threads," I said. I didn't know if this was his first name, his second name or his title. "Threads," I said again, to get used to it.

"You can start straight away," Threads said. "And find yourself summat to wear out of stock." He peered at me with a slight look of disgust in his eyes. "You look more like a boot boy than a shop boy."

"Yes, Threads," I said. How right he was – and how easily I'd fooled him.

By the end of that day I was all settled in. I spent the afternoon rummaging through the piles of old clothes and found a tight bodice to hide my shape, and two linen shirts. Then I picked out a smart brown suit from the back of a pile marked "Gents Best" and went behind a tattered curtain to put them all on. I felt I shouldn't wear my flat cap in the shop, but since Threads didn't seem to be bothered either way, I left it on as part of my disguise.

When I was all kitted out, I felt rather pleased with myself. For the rest of the day I patrolled the front of the shop on the look-out for customers. There weren't too many of these, for most of the men who came in the shop seemed intent on some other, private business with Threads.

I looked out on the lane, at the travelling chair-menders, the organist with his monkey and the penny peddlers, and I saw the dark-haired blind girl again. She carried a bowl and a white stick, as before. There was a purple bruise on her cheekbone, and I wondered if she'd got it when her father had pushed her onto the floor of his cart.

I watched how she worked. As she heard people pass by, she held out the bowl she carried and tap-tapped on the cobbles with her stick to draw attention to herself. "Help a poor blind girl," she would call over to them. "Please spare a ha'penny for a blind girl!"

Very few people gave her money, for I had already realised that this was a very poor part of London, and not many *had* a spare ha'penny. But I saw that she sounded desperate and looked very pale, and I made up my mind that the next time I had a coin in my pocket she should have it.

CHAPTER 6

A week or so later I saw the blind girl at the bottom of Pudding Lane. That's where the fire started almost two hundred years ago – the great fire which burned down thousands of houses and many fine old churches. The girl came up from the direction of the river, tip-tapping her cane and turning towards those who passed her with her usual call.

I noticed that she seemed to know whether those she addressed were men or women. This didn't surprise me, for they do say that if you lose one of your senses, then the others work harder to make up for the one that's missing.

I stood still and waited until she got close to me, then I bade her a good morning.

She replied in kind and bobbed a curtsey, and then she added, "Kind sir, please could you spare a coin for a blind girl?"

I was pleased that the girl's instincts seemed to tell her that I was a boy, but I was sad that I had to disappoint her.

"I'm afraid I have no money," I said. Threads had sent me out to get bread and cheese for our dinner, but he had an account in the shop and so I had no money on me. I looked down at the loaf in my hand. "If you're hungry," I said, "I could spare some of this bread ..."

She didn't reply.

"But perhaps you're not hungry ..." I began.

"Oh, I am, sir!" she said. She thought for a moment then added, "You see, my father doesn't allow me to accept food. He thinks I work better when I have a hunger upon me." Her voice was bitter.

"Then hurry and take this," I said, and I broke the loaf and put half in her hands. "I'll tell my master that I've already eaten my piece."

She smiled. The first smile I'd seen from her. "Tis most kind of you," she said. She put as much as was polite into her mouth and chewed for some time before she spoke again.

I studied her face as she ate. Her long dark hair fell across her face and almost hid the bruise on her cheek, and there was a sore patch on her forehead.

"Who's your master?" she asked when she'd eaten a fair amount. "Are you apprenticed to someone in the city?"

"I work in the second-hand clothes business," I said, and I felt rather proud. "My master calls himself Threads."

Her head jerked up. "Threads?" she repeated, and I couldn't tell from the tone of her voice whether she approved of him or not. "My father sometimes works with him."

"Is your father in the clothing business, then?" I asked.

She gave a shiver. "He's in every business," she said. "Every *dark* business."

I looked again at the bruises on her face. "Have you no mother to protect you?"

She shook her head. "My mother died giving birth to me."

"Mine too!" I said. It was odd, but I was glad that we had this in common, for I was eager to become her friend.

"My aunt in Dorset wished for me to go and live with her, but my father had a better idea," she told me. "He knew that a poor blind child would make good money as a beggar."

I looked at her with some pity but, of course, she couldn't see this.

"As soon as I could walk, he had me go begging." She touched my arm. "Young sir, I thank you for the bread, but I must move on."

"Twas nothing," I told her.

"Will you tell me your name?"

I was so lost in my pity for her, that I nearly said my real name, but I remembered in time to say that it was George.

"And mine is Anna."

She gave me a quick, shy smile and then we parted – me to go back to Threads with half a loaf, and she to resume her dreary round of the city.

My master didn't realise that part of his loaf was missing, because when I got back to the shop he was deep in conversation with three rough-looking men. They were all talking in low, excited voices about some deal or other. They went off to the Green Man as soon as I was back behind the counter.

I was pleased to be on my own and I set to tidying the shop, which I admit is a very feminine activity, but I could not seem to stop myself. It was a ridiculous task and nearly impossible, because of the huge amount of clothes that were flung everywhere. There were coats, cloaks, suits, dresses, jackets, trousers and the like, and smaller things too – nightgowns and socks, scarves, shawls, handkerchiefs and shoes. All of these were in very different states. Some were clean and tidy, almost new, and some were fit only to become household rags.

In between tidying, I served two customers – one bought a plain cotton petticoat and the other, a woollen scarf. Threads had said nothing as to what price these – or any other – garments should be, so I sold each for tuppence and hoped that was right.

Darkness fell and just as I was wondering if I should close the shop, Threads arrived back with his mates. They were all the worse for wear. They ignored me and went to the back of the shop where they passed a bottle of gin around, becoming more and more drunk. A bit later, I was thinking of climbing under the counter and trying to get to sleep when Threads lurched his way down from the back of the shop.

"Everyone must drink to our success!" he said. His words were blurred and he was swaying on his feet. "Everyone! Even my new shop boy."

I tried to refuse, but he insisted. He thrust the bottle at me and I pretended to take a swig. Even the smell made me feel sick. Of course, I hid this, for I didn't want to show any female frailty.

But Threads didn't give up so easy. "You've not taken enough, George!" he said. "You must drink to us as if you mean it!"

He took the bottle back and poured some of the gin into a cup which he pressed to my lips.

"Get it down you!" he said.

The others gathered around and clapped while I retched and coughed. I finished the cup to loud cheers.

A moment later, I felt the room swing about me. Sick and dizzy, I closed my eyes and edged along the counter to my sleeping place. When I reached it, I dropped like a stone into it.

"He's not a lad who can take his grog!" I heard Threads say.

'He's not a *lad* at all,' I thought – and then I fell into darkness.

 CHAPTER 7

When I woke up it was just before midnight, for
I heard the church clock strike the hour. I had
a terrible taste in my mouth and I longed for a
glass of water – even Thames water – but I could
not bring myself to move from my burrow. I put
out my hand and discovered, to my disgust, that
I must have been sick sometime in the night. I
made an attempt to get up, but my legs refused
to obey me. I told myself that I'd sort everything
out in the morning.

I looked about me in the darkness, sick and
weary and still half-drunk, and I could hardly
work out where I was. Outside in the lane
someone was waving a lantern, and a pattern of
shadows and light swung about the shop, so that
I felt even more giddy. I looked up. Everything
about me seemed to have taken on a different,
more menacing appearance. A row of old shirts
flew above me, their arms pinned out like angels'

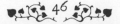

wings, and there was a line of jackets on hangers, looming over me like sleeping bats. I felt pressed down and threatened by the old clothes. It seemed that they might flap down and smother me if I fell asleep.

I heard voices outside and I realised that these must have woken me. Threads was there, speaking in a low, angry voice, and someone was replying in kind. There was a tussle, a couple of shouts of pain and a cry of something like, "Spider! Get the stiff off the street!"

After the cry, the shop door flew open with such a crash it was a wonder the glass didn't break. Then I heard three or four pairs of heavy boots clatter across the wooden floor and some swearing from Threads.

I huddled under my blanket. If I kept quiet, perhaps they wouldn't remember I was there. Perhaps they'd go away and I could calm my raging headache and go back to sleep. Had Threads put something else in my drink, I wondered, to make me feel as bad as I did right then?

The men were only in the shop a matter of moments – just long enough to carry in something that looked like a large bundle of garments and push it under the counter on the other side of the shop. Then they ran out again and slammed the door behind them, and I heard nothing more. My eyes closed and I went back into a heavy and befuddled sleep.

Further into the night, perhaps two or three o'clock, I woke and realised I needed to be sick again. This time, for all I was weak as a kitten, I lit a candle and managed to get into the yard before my stomach emptied itself.

Afterwards my legs trembled and I had to clutch onto the wall for support as I made my way back into the shop. I felt so ill, but I still couldn't resist going to look under the far counter of the shop. What had all the fuss been about? Had Threads and his cronies robbed another clothes shop and returned with some valuable garments – furs and evening clothes, perhaps?

But what I saw under the counter terrified me, for lying there, stretched out, was a dead body.

It was the corpse of a man with grey hair and a moustache. He was half-wrapped in a winding sheet, with his hands folded across his chest.

I burst into tears of fright and ran back to my own little sleeping spot. A corpse! I was sharing a room with a corpse.

I didn't want to be a smart lad any longer! Why had I *ever* left Rose Villa? I wept for a while, but then at last, as my body still churned with the effects of whatever I'd been given to drink, I fell asleep.

When I woke again it was light and I had a thumping headache, but I no longer felt sick. I lay still for a moment or two, thinking of what had happened the night before ... and then I remembered the corpse under the counter.

No, it was not possible. I must have imagined it. It must have been a nightmare caused by the drink ...

I climbed out of my cubby-hole, careful not to move my head around too much, and made my way to the far counter.

There was nothing there.

 49

I drew in my breath with a shudder. Of course there was nothing there! It had been a horrible dream, just as I'd thought. But what about the men shouting outside, the crash of the shop door, the bundle they had carried in? Had that *all* been a dream?

I pondered on this as I went into the yard and splashed my face. Then I returned to the shop with a rag and cleaned up where I'd been sick. I looked under the far counter again. It was still empty, of course, and there was nothing that shouldn't have been there, just a rather mouldy, decaying sort of smell. But that didn't mean anything – all sorts of rotten smells came in from the Thames at high tide.

Threads didn't come in that morning. He'd already told me that if he didn't turn up then I should work the shop on my own, and that's what I did. I sold a lace petticoat to an old woman and a straw hat to a bald-headed man. I couldn't help but tidy up some more too, and that was when I found the source of the mouldy smell. It came from something I hadn't seen before – a gentleman's evening suit, rather old-fashioned, with velvet lapels and purple silk lining.

Well into the afternoon, Threads appeared, unshaven and grey of face. I was all set to ask him about the fuss of the night before, but he was in a vile mood and sent me straight out to the Waterman's Arms for a pint of Strong, so I thought it best not to mention it.

Outside the Waterman's Arms, which was right on the river and very run-down and seedy, I found my friend Anna. She had her white stick and begging bowl, and she looked very sorry for herself.

"It's me – George," I said, and I wished that I had a penny or two to put in her bowl.

Her face lit up for a moment and I thought how pretty she was, in spite of the bruises across her cheek.

"I can't stay for long today," I said. "My master was out all night and he came in just now with a foul temper upon him."

"So did my father!" she said. "The two of them were out on a job together, you know. They call my father Spider."

"Yes," I said. "I heard the two of them arguing." I hesitated. "But what business are they in?"

"Don't you know?"

I shook my head, then I realised she couldn't see me and so I said that I had no idea.

"They're in the body trade," Anna said.

"The body trade?" I repeated. I didn't understand what she meant.

"Yes. Threads and my father steal dead people from graveyards."

I gasped and my stomach tipped and churned once more. "But why?"

A slight smile crossed Anna's face. "You're a lad who's not been in London long, that's for sure," she said in a clear, low voice. "Have you not heard of the body snatchers?"

CHAPTER 8

"Body snatchers?" I stuttered. "Well – yes, but ..."

Anna shook her head at my ignorance, but there was no smile on her face any more.

"Threads and Spider hear of a funeral of someone rich, and a night or two later the two of them go to the graveyard and dig up the coffin," she told me. "They force it open and Spider takes the body to sell to the hospital doctors, while Threads gets the clothes."

I shuddered at the thought.

"Then they fight between them over any rings, watches or other bits they find buried with the corpse." Anna gave a shiver. "One time they found a silver teapot. Another time a diamond ring was buried with a young bride. *That* caused a terrible fight." She took a breath. "Last night something went wrong. The constables turned up half way through the job and there wasn't time to get the corpse off to hospital."

I gasped. "Get the stiff off the street," I told her. "I heard them say that."

"That's right," she told me. "My father said they had to hide the body in case the constables caught them with him, so they took him into Threads' shop and shoved him under the counter."

"I knew it!" I shivered. "I saw the corpse! I thought it was a nightmare, but it can't have been ..."

"They collected him later, when the coast was clear," she said. "I worried you might wake up and wonder what was going on, but then I thought you must have slept right through it."

"No, I woke up a couple of times and – oh! – then I found a gentleman's dress suit with purple satin lining," I said. "He must have been wearing that in the coffin."

"And there's a black silk top hat," Anna said.

"But how do you know all this?"

"Because I was there in the graveyard," she said. "Spider makes me sit in the cart and keep watch."

I stared at her in surprise. "Keep watch?" I echoed in surprise. "But you ..."

"I have very good hearing. I can hear a watchman calling seven streets away. And besides," she said, and a bitter note tainted her voice, "someone has to be there to do the dirty work. It's me who has to strip the bodies of their clothes, take the rings off their fingers and the shoes from their feet."

I flinched at the thought of her feeling her way around the corpses to do this grisly work. "Don't you mind doing that?" I asked.

"Of course I mind! I hate it!"

"Then can't you say to your father that you'd rather not?"

Her bottom lip trembled and a tear seeped from under a closed eyelid. "Say that to Spider?" she said. "Tell him I don't want to do it any more? He'd take *my* body to the hospital."

I squeezed her hand, feeling very sorry for her. But I couldn't forget that Threads was back at the shop waiting for his beer, so I said goodbye and promised that I'd come and look for her whenever I could.

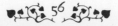

Our paths met again two days later. Threads had sent me to buy pipe tobacco and I saw Anna, looking cold and unhappy, tap-tapping up to Lombard's Market. Two urchins of five or six years of age were following her. They crept beside her on silent bare feet and tried to startle her by crying "Boo!" and "Yah!" at her. I caught up with them, grabbed them by their collars and told them to scram.

Anna turned to me and smiled. "George, thank you. Usually I can chase them off on my own, but today I can't seem to find the strength."

I asked her why not, but she turned away. "Tis nothing," she muttered.

I touched her arm. "Aren't we friends?" I said. "Maybe I can do something to help you."

Mary Hooper

She shook her head. "You can't."

"Please ..."

I wouldn't leave it and at last she said in a low voice, "Spider says I'm not bringing in enough money and I must sell my hair."

"*No!*" I cried in horror.

I'd seen, of course, the man in Lombard's Market who bought poor girls' hair to make into wigs. Long fair hair was the most prized, but locks like Anna's, as dark and shiny as a new chestnut, were almost as much in demand.

"I'm on my way now to O'Leary in the market," she told me. "Spider said I must ask for no less than two shillings and bring the money back right away."

As I looked at her face, sadder than ever, I felt a sudden storm of rage at her father.

She gave a sob. "He will shave it right to the scalp and I will be as bald as the old men who sit outside taverns wearing sleeping caps to keep their heads warm!"

"And what if you refuse to have it done?" I asked.

She shrugged. "If I don't come home with two shillings, he swears he'll sell me off to the highest bidder."

"*Sell* you?"

"There are plenty of men who'd marry me in order to send me out to beg," she said.

"Wait! I'll try and get the money for you," I said. The words tumbled out in my haste to save her. "I'll ask Threads for a loan."

"Threads!" she cried. "He'll never ..."

But I was away. I dodged past the peddlers and the market stalls, burst into the grocer's to buy the tobacco and then ran back to the clothes shop as fast as I could. Here I found my master pacing around the place, keen to be gone and angry because I'd been too long over the errand. He left in such a rush, in fact, that I had no chance to ask him if I could have some of my wages early.

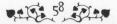

'I'll just have to "borrow" it,' I thought. It was a good job that I'd sold a couple of garments and there was money in the tin box under the counter.

# CHAPTER 9

I raced back to the market and found O'Leary. He stood between a hulk of a man waving a pair of pliers with which he pulled out teeth, and one selling cream to get rid of freckles.

There were three girls waiting to have their heads shaved, and all of them were crying. I felt desperately sorry for them, for selling your hair was the last step on the road to becoming a pauper, a complete down-and-out. No girl would suffer to do it unless she was starving. Or, like Anna, because she'd been forced into it by someone who should have protected her.

O'Leary's stall was nothing more than an old trestle table. On it was a pair of brass scales and a notice.

HUMAN HAIR BOUGHT

Must be clean.

Minimum length eight inches.

One penny per ounce.

I stood and watched for a moment. One girl was sitting on a stool with her fair hair loose and down to her waist. She was crying as O'Leary divided her hair into clumps and tied it. Then, with an instrument like a razor which went close to the scalp, he began to shear her like a lamb at Smithfield. He tied each lock with cotton, put it on the scales and noted down its weight before he shaved off the next piece.

Anna was next in line, and I went to her and took her hand. "It's me," I said. "It's all right. You don't have to do this."

"George!" She turned to me in tears, and took in a breath like a sob. "I have to! Or would you rather have me marry an old man with the stink of beer on his breath and no teeth?"

"Of course I wouldn't! Look, I've borrowed the money for you," I said, and I gave her a handful of copper coins.

She gasped in surprise. "So Threads lent ..."

"Threads knows nothing about it," I said in a low voice. "I got the money from the box under the counter – I'll pay it back when I get my wages."

"Oh!"

For a moment Anna looked quite overcome, and I thought she was going to start crying again. In this pause I could hear the scrape of O'Leary's razor as he took the last lock of hair from the fair girl's head.

Anna squeezed my hand. "George – I can't believe you've done this for me."

"Of course I have. I can't be seen with a friend who has no hair!" I joked. I knew that I really should tell her my secret. 'If I'm to be best friends with a girl,' I thought, 'then that girl should know if I'm male or female.'

O'Leary had paid off the fair girl with a few coins and he was looking at Anna, and her thick glossy hair. The spark in his eye made me flinch. "Next!" he cried. "Come and take a seat, my dear."

"Not today, thank you!" I said, and I pulled Anna out of the line.

She still hesitated. "But ... are you sure ...?"

"Yes!" I squeezed her hand. "Go home and give the money to your father. I must get back to the shop to try to sell some clothes."

We walked out of the market, Anna's white cane tapping in a half-circle before her. She didn't have her begging bowl with her, but two people pressed small coins into her hand.

"No one's ever done anything like that for me before," Anna said. "And in exchange I must tell you a secret."

"Not now!" I said.

I feared she was going to make some sort of declaration of best-friendship to me. I would have been happy to hear this at any other time, but right then I needed to get back to the shop in case Threads returned and discovered I was missing.

"When we have more time, then," she said. She kissed me on the cheek, thanked me once again, and we parted.

It had started to rain by the time I got back, and the rain turned to an icy sleet which I knew would keep any customers at home. All the same, I stood for a while under the shop's tattered awning and tried to entice passers-by.

"Come in out of the rain!" I called, and, "Buy your wet weather clothes here!" But none of the housewives even looked my way as they hurried home from market.

I jiggled the tin box, which was supposed to contain a float of money. I had to hope that Threads wouldn't look in there, because all that was in it now was a penny from the sale of a hat the day before.

By nine o'clock that evening I hadn't had a single customer over the threshold. I was very weary, and I decided to go to my bed. I yawned as I took off my cap, went to check that the front doors of the shop were locked and turned the sign in the window from "Open" to "Closed".

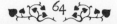

As I did this, I saw someone move outside in the street. I stared out the window and, to my horror, I found myself looking straight into the face of Jameson the boot boy.

I prayed that my face hadn't revealed the shock I felt. I managed to control myself long enough to bellow, "We're closed now!" in my deepest voice. I followed this with a manly "Goodnight to you, sir!" before I turned away.

Jameson didn't respond to either of these statements. He just stood there gawping, as if he couldn't believe his eyes.

I put my hands in my pockets and went to the back of the shop, whistling as though I didn't have a care in the world. But that night I couldn't sleep for fear. If I knew Jameson, he'd be back in the morning to check on what he'd seen.

# CHAPTER 10

Opposite the clothes shop was an old brick wall, stuck all over with tattered posters and adverts. When there were no customers in the shop – which was often – I'd stand and stare at the adverts. These were for everything you can think of – from baby food

Make your baby as fat as a pig!

to headache cures

Absolutely safe and acts like Magic

and beauty creams

Recommended for the skin by Mrs Langtree.

A couple of days after I'd given the two shillings to Anna, I saw that a new poster had been pasted up.

RUNAWAYS!

The apprentices named hereunder have absconded from their places of work and broken their Bonds with their Masters. If anyone has knowledge of the whereabouts of Tommy Hogg, Albert Scuttle or Peter James, believed to be working in the building trade, or Georgina Friday, a kitchen maid, you are obliged to let the Parish know immediately. A reward is offered.

I began shaking all over when I read this. But I gave myself a talking-to, telling myself that I was a long way from Rose Villa. And of course I was no longer Gina but George, a smart lad who was a sales assistant in a second-hand clothes shop. And as long as Jameson didn't put two and two together, I'd be all right.

All the same, I didn't like looking at that poster, so when Threads wasn't around I went out and scratched at it with a fork so that my name was gone. I couldn't help wondering what the authorities would do if they found me out. Would

I be sent to a workhouse – I was too old now to live in an orphanage – or would I receive a jail sentence with hard labour, or be transported as a convict to one of the colonies on the other side of the world? Each one of those three options seemed worse than the last.

I worked hard over the next two or three days and sold a good few garments, which replaced the two shillings I'd borrowed to give Anna. I also decided that Spider and Threads must have another big job coming up, for Anna's father came into the shop a couple of times to mutter and plot with Threads behind the back counter. Each time he ignored my respectful *"Good morning, sir."*

One day I had to take some clothes to sell on a stall run by one of Threads' mates in Petticoat Lane. The fellow was dressed in a muddle of old finery and a tall, very shiny top hat. As I left the garments with him, I remarked that the market seemed very quiet. It was usually heaving with people.

"What's happened?" I asked him. "Where's everyone gone?"

Mary Hooper

"Oh, it's the funeral of some big-wig down at St Alfred's."

"Is he important?"

"He's stinking rich!" he said. "London folk love a big funeral, see. Some of them will have been waiting all night to get a place at the front of the crowds."

His words made me long to see this sight, so when I left him I followed a group of apprentices with black ribbons tied around their upper arms. Soon I caught up with a dozen carriages with lowered blinds, all heading for St Alfred's Church. Here two hundred or more folk had gathered, eager to see the gentry in all their finery. The owners of the carriages climbed out at the church door, treating the onlookers to a display of the most lavish and fashionable mourning clothes. They wore gorgeous gowns in black silks and satins and extravagant hats swathed in fine black veils.

A magnificent black stallion pulled the final carriage, which was made of glass. This held the coffin and what looked like hundreds of white lilies. When the back of the carriage was opened

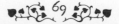

so that the body could be carried into the church, the sickly perfume from these flowers filled the air.

I looked around and marvelled at the scene – the gentry in their deepest mourning, the fine horses in head-dresses with plumes of black feathers, great heaps of lilies, roses and laurel, and a line of old men carrying velvet cushions holding the dead man's medals.

What a funeral!

I thought of Anna and wished she could see it too. Of course she could not – but what a tale I'd have to tell her.

When the church doors closed on the last of the mourners, I raced back to the shop.

"Sorry I'm late," I said to Threads. Then, when I'd caught my breath, I told him about all I'd seen at the funeral – the smart carriages, the elegant ladies and the general air of wealth.

"In time, lad," he said, "some of them mourning clothes will end up in this shop to be sold." Then he added, in quite a calm voice, "But right now, I expect you're hoping I won't say anything about those two shillings you've stolen from my cash box."

I started gabbling my excuses in dismay, telling him about how upset a friend of mine had been at the thought of selling her hair. "I only borrowed it because of her," I said. "I wasn't going to keep it. I was going to pay you back when I got my wages."

He looked at me and raised one eyebrow.

"I swear!" I said. "I took it as a loan."

"Well," he said. "We'll have to think of a way you can return it, won't we?"

"Couldn't I re-pay it bit by bit from my wages?"

He shook his head. "I think I'll give you a special task – one that will wipe out your debt in full."

I nodded. "I'd be very happy to –"

"But if you don't want to do this task," he cut in, "then I'm sorry but I'll have to hand you over to the constables. Stealing from your employer is a hanging crime, you know."

"No need for you to tell the constables, sir!" I gabbled. "What is it you want me to do?"

He gave me a strange smile. "Let's just say it's a little night work."

"*Night work*," I repeated.

"A collection and delivery service," he said, and the smirk stretched right across his face.

My heart plummeted. I knew exactly what kind of night work it was that he was talking about.

❧

"A collection and delivery service," I repeated to Anna. I knew her usual route through the lanes now, and I had gone round by the Green Man in the hope I would meet up with her. "I know what that means – they want me to collect and deliver a dead body."

Anna nodded. "And I know whose body it will be – the man who was laid to rest today in St Alfred's churchyard."

I gasped. "I saw his funeral!" I looked at her again. There was a new bruise on her forehead and her face was so pale that I could almost see through the skin. "But, Anna, you don't look well ..."

She shook her head as if to dismiss my worries. "Spider's keeping me hungry – he thinks I'll earn more money if I look ill."

"How do you stand it?"

She shrugged. "I've been wondering these last few days if I could run away. I could go to the docks and get a job as a washerwoman on board a boat. Or there's going to be a Great Exhibition next year – have you heard? – and they want all sorts of people to work there."

"But ..." I wondered how a blind girl would get any job at all, but I couldn't bring myself to say it.

"If I run away, why don't you come with me?" she asked. "You'd get work at this Great

Exhibition as easy as anything. Boys can do so many more jobs than girls."

"Do you think so?" I said, and my heart started to race as fast as one of the new steam trains. It would have been a perfect time to tell her that her chum George was, in fact, a girl named Georgina. But I was a coward, and I couldn't bring myself to do it for fear she might no longer want to be friends. And so I put it off until further notice.

CHAPTER 11

Three nights later I was sitting in a cart in a quiet side street near St Alfred's Church, yawning over and over while we waited for Threads and Spider to decide if the moon was going to stay behind the clouds. If it *was*, then they reckoned it would be safe to remove the corpse from what he had thought would be his final resting place. Anna had told me that they usually had two young men there to help with the digging, but they'd refused to come because the penalties for grave-robbing were now so severe.

"Word has it that our man has been buried with all his medals, two gold pocket-watches and a signet ring," she'd told me the day before. "And neither of those two greedy toads can resist the idea of so much gold."

The last two nights had gone by in much the same way – me and Anna sitting for hours in the cart beside Spider and Threads, until the two men decided that there wasn't enough cloud to cover the moon and any passing constable might be able to spot them. Tonight was the last chance to retrieve the corpse, for Anna had told me the hospitals liked the bodies to be no more than ten days dead, and our man had already spent a week waiting for his funeral to be held.

As I sat there, I felt numb, cold and miserable. I hated the idea of what I had to do and I feared that now there would be no escape from the two body-snatchers' clutches – Threads would demand my help on every job from now on. I was troubled, too, because, in the market the day before, I thought I'd seen Jameson lurking on every street corner. It never turned out to be him, but that didn't stop me fearing that every weasel-faced apprentice in London was out to get me. Had Jameson seen through my disguise or not?

The clouds shifted again, and Threads and Spider went off to make another check on the graveyard. Anna was left in the front of the cart to hold the reins of the horse. I was about to whisper to her when Threads came running back.

"The job's on – bring the pickaxe," he said in an urgent whisper to me, and he took a spade and a heavy crowbar from the back of the cart.

My heart sank even further. I'd been hoping that they'd just brought me along to drive the cart, but it was clear they expected me to wield a pickaxe too. I feared I'd be useless at this grim task, for despite all the heavy domestic work I'd done at Rose Villa I could hardly lift the thing, let alone swing it up over my shoulder and down into the hard earth.

"Good luck," Anna said in the smallest of whispers, as soon as Threads had pounded off again. "I'll be listening out for you."

"Thanks." I looked at her in despair, but I could say nothing more.

The pickaxe was too heavy to carry over my shoulder – as I'd known it would be – so as I walked into the graveyard I began to drag it along the path behind me. I'd never been in a graveyard after dark before, and I did not much enjoy the experience. There had been a fog earlier that day which had left pockets of soft mist, and there were dripping leaves and spiders' webs brushing against my face as I walked. It was all I could do not to throw down the pickaxe and run back out the gates as fast as I could.

Under the twisted yew trees I could see the dim shapes of gravestones, family vaults, and mighty buildings flanked by weeping stone angels and built for several generations of the same family. Some of the smaller graves had lanterns placed on them, so I knew that the dead person's next of kin must come regularly with fresh candles. The tiny flames from these lanterns shimmered and danced, and lit up stone cherubs, covered urns, broken columns and all the most fashionable mourning sculptures.

As I looked about me in fear, the evening star shone out in a spark of silver that let me see Threads on the path ahead of me and Spider, further off, waiting by a newly dug mound of earth.

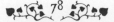

Mary Hooper

The graves were very close to each other and digging was difficult. I was useless, as I'd known I would be, but Threads and Spider were men more used to hard drinking than hard labour, and they weren't a lot better.

After fifteen minutes of digging, Threads was wheezing and struggling to draw breath. "Going to sit in the cart for a minute," he said. He picked up one of the two lanterns in order to see his way across to the cart. "You two go on digging."

We carried on for several minutes until Spider threw down his spade. "Know what?" he said. "You're no use at all. No more help than a girl."

I believe a slight smile crossed my face – something maddened him anyway, because as I stood up, he punched me hard in the arm. "Go and get Threads," he ordered. "Tell him to get back here now."

The force of his punch threw me onto the family crypt next door to the plot we were working on. I was winded, and I stayed on the ground for a moment. I felt a sudden murderous rage towards Spider, this tyrant, this *bully* who starved and beat up his own daughter.

I feared now that he was going to beat me up, too, and I grabbed the other lantern. I didn't have a clear plan of action but I saw that the door of the family tomb was open, and I slipped inside and hid behind a marble shelf that held two coffins. When Spider blundered down the steps, yelling he was going to teach me a lesson, I was well placed to give him a hefty kick in the backside and send him sprawling across the paved floor.

Quick as a flash I went back up the steps and back outside. Then I took hold of the handle and pulled the door towards me with as much strength as I could muster. It shut with a solid click, leaving me outside with the lantern and Spider trapped inside in the dark.

"Come back here, you bloody useless blighter! Open this door!" I heard his muffled voice yell, as I brushed the dirt from my trousers. "You'll be sorry for this!"

I didn't wait to hear any more threats. I left the tools where they were and ran back to

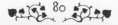

the cart. When I reached it, I saw the relief on Anna's face when she realised it was me and not her father who'd returned.

"Spider wants you!" I gasped to Threads, who was sitting beside Anna. "We dug down as far as the coffin, but he can't open it."

"What? The fella's got a crowbar, ain't he?" Threads wheezed as he climbed out of the cart. "He's just sent you away so he can bag the gold watches himself. You should never have left him, you stupid oaf!"

I hung my head, doing my best to look confused and apologetic.

"Put a new candle in the other lantern and then follow me back," Threads demanded.

I waited until he'd disappeared into the graveyard's hazy mists, and then I climbed onto the cart next to Anna. She looked puzzled, but she turned her head in my direction. Her expression said, *What next?*

"Walk on!" I said. "Walk on!"

Anna repeated this to the horse and, with a flick of the reins, it began to walk forward.

"George, whatever's happened?" she asked, looking over her shoulder in fear.

I took a deep breath. "Well, first of all, the two of them are never going to get that coffin out – it's buried much too deep. Second, I've shut Spider in a family tomb with a couple of old coffins for company!"

She gasped, then laughed.

"He's not going to get out of there any time soon – and when he does, the family who own the tomb are going to be very keen to know just what he was doing there."

"Oh – perfect!" she cried, and clapped her hands. "That'll teach him!"

"Threads is going to be in a bit of a fix, too," I went on, unable to hide the glee in my voice, "because it's getting on for daylight and he's in a graveyard with two pickaxes, a spade, a crowbar and no way of getting away. It's not going to look good when the watchman does his rounds."

As the horse plodded its steady way along the streets, and the city came to life all around us, we began to breathe more easily.

"But where are we going now?" Anna asked.

"Well, you told me that you had an aunt in Dorset," I said. "I wondered if we could go there."

Anna nodded, excited. "Of course," she said. "She'll be so pleased to think I've got away from *him*."

"So, let's go," I said, full of excitement. "I don't know the way to Dorset but we can head south-west towards Salisbury and ask our way from there." I looked at Anna. "I'd better take over the reins, I think."

"No, I'll be fine," Anna said.

"But – you can't see. We'll have an accident!"

She laughed. "That's what I've been wanting to tell you. George – haven't you noticed? I'm not blind."

"*What?!*"

The horse picked up a little speed, and its hooves made a happy sound as they covered the cobbles, each *clip-clop* taking us further away from Spider, Threads and our old lives.

"But …"

"You see, as soon as I could walk, Spider forced me to pretend I was blind, carry a white stick and keep my eyes closed whenever I was out of the house." Her voice sank. "No one else knows the truth. He said he'd kill me if I ever told anyone."

I looked at her as I tried to take this in. I waved my hand in front of her face and with a laugh, she caught hold of it.

"It's true!" she cried. Her eyes – they were deep brown – sparkled. "Honestly. I really can see you, George!"

I swallowed. I had my own story to tell, but I didn't know where to start.

"I was thinking," she said, before I'd got my words together, "they'll be looking for a girl and a boy, but not two girls. Why don't we dress you up as a girl?"

Surprised, I made a little sound of protest.

Anna studied my face with a frown. "If you grew your hair," she said, "I think you'd make quite a decent girl." Then, in a teasing tone, she said, "You'd look very fine in a skirt!"

I began to laugh.

"No, really, George," Anna said. "I think it might be a good idea."

"Mmmm ..." I took a deep breath. "Well, before you start dressing me up, there's something I need to tell you, too."

She looked at me curiously. "Whatever it is, we're still going to be friends, aren't we?"

"Yes," I said. "I do believe we are ..."

And, laughing again, we drove through the city gates and took the turnpike road towards Dorset and the new life that awaited both of us.

MARY HOOPER has written lots of brilliant historical novels, including ...

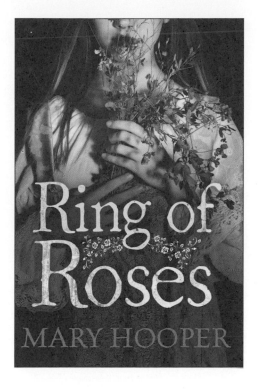

London, 1665

Abby is very pleased with her new position as nursemaid to baby Grace in the grand house of Belle Vue. She loves the sights, sounds and tastes of the big city, from her friend Hannah's sweet treats to days out among the rich at the Royal Exchange.

But then the rumours begin, the bells toll and houses all across the city are boarded up. The Plague has come to London. Can Abby and Hannah escape its clutches?

www.barringtonstoke.co.uk

Our books are tested
for children and young people by
children and young people.

Thanks to everyone who consulted on
a manuscript for their time and effort in
helping us to make our books better
for our readers.